The Barefoot Book of
MONStErS!

Barefoot Books
Celebrating Art and Story

For Mum, Dad and Liam, with monster amounts of love; and for Suzanne,
for being a pal and posting things — F. P.

To my friend Andrea — S. F.

Barefoot Books
2067 Massachusetts Ave
Cambridge, MA 02140

This book was typeset in Gilligan's Island and Skia
The illustrations were prepared in watercolor

Graphic design by Applecart, England
Color separation by Bright Arts, Singapore
Printed and bound in China by Printplus Ltd

This book has been printed on 100% acid-free paper

ISBN 978-1-84148-178-4

3 5 7 9 8 6 4 2

The Barefoot Book of

MONSTERS!

Retold by Fran Parnell

Illustrated by Sophie Fatus

CONTENTS

THE TERRIBLE CHENOO

Micmac/Passamaquoddy — North American

ONE AUTUMN way back at the beginning of the world, a husband and wife left their tribe to go hunting in the northwest. They found a pleasant clearing in the pine forest and set up their tepee to spend the winter there. Every day, the man went off to hunt while his wife dressed and dried the meat so that they would have plenty to eat over the long winter. All went well for a time; game was plentiful, the weather was fine and the husband and wife were happy in the little glade.

One crisp autumn day, while the man was away hunting, the woman went to gather more wood for the fire. The sudden whistle of an icy wind and a strange rustling sound in the bushes close by made her look up. A dreadful sight met her eyes, for there, glaring at her, was an old and evil Chenoo. He had the eyes of a starving wolf and his teeth were as sharp and pointed as a bear's. He was as old as the earth and in his chest beat a cruel and ancient heart, colder than ice. The Chenoo had traveled from the far north land, flying on the frosty wind, and the long journey had made him hungry, starving, ravenous, for a bite of juicy meat.

The woman trembled all over with fear. But she was as sharp as a fox, this woman, and had no plans to end her days as a Chenoo's meal. Thinking quickly, she flung down her firewood, and with a gasp of surprise and a hoot of joy, she threw her arms around the old Chenoo and gave him a great big hug.

"Father!" she cried. "What a wonderful surprise! How well you look! And how good of you to travel all this way to visit us!"

Then she held the savage creature at arm's length and looked him up and down, while a puzzled look crossed her face. "But what has happened to your clothes, Father? You must be frozen through! Come into the tepee and warm yourself up." And, chattering away, she took hold of the monster's hand and led him out of the bushes.

The Chenoo was very surprised. He had eaten plenty of people before, and usually they screamed, or tried to run off, or fainted clean away before he gobbled them up. The Chenoo was so surprised, in fact, that he forgot to eat the woman. He was so astonished that he followed the woman meekly into the tepee. He was so amazed that he let the woman dress him in a deerskin shirt, leather breeches and a fine pair of moccasins, until he was wrapped up as snugly as a baby in a papoose.

"There now, Father, isn't that better?" said the woman briskly. "With a good bright blaze, your old bones will be warm again in no time. I'll just go and collect some sticks to build up the fire."

8

The woman scurried out of the tepee, but her knees were soon knocking again, for the terrible Chenoo picked up an axe and followed her outside.

"By the Wise Old One!" the woman exclaimed. "He means to chop me up!"

But the Chenoo began to chop down the tall forest trees instead. He chopped and he chopped, and the great pine trees toppled around him as quickly as if he was cutting down blades of grass. He had chopped down half the forest before the woman was able to gather her wits and her breath and shout, "Father! We have enough wood now!"

Without a word, the Chenoo began to collect up the fallen trees and pile them up neatly behind the tepee. Just then, the woman saw her husband coming, picking his way over the tree trunks and looking about him in amazement. Before the monster saw him, the woman quickly explained what had happened, so, as her husband walked up to the Chenoo, he was able to cry, "Father-in-law! How kind of you to journey all this way to see us! I have caught enough food today for us to have a splendid meal while you tell us all the news from home!"

9

The Chenoo remained sullen and silent when they all sat down to feast. Although the husband and wife were still terrified of the monster, they ate heartily and chatted about their tribe. They gossiped about the neighbors and wondered together what their family and their friends were doing at that moment, and whether they were all safe and well.

Although the man and woman offered the monster fresh caribou meat, spirals of dried pumpkin and hot corn coffee, the Chenoo did not eat. Instead, he listened carefully to the conversation, and gradually a gentle look came over his monstrous face. He had never had a family or any friends. In his home in the far north, the Chenoos attacked one another whenever they met. With terrible screams, they grew huge with rage until their heads touched the clouds. Then they would fight for days and days until the sky thundered and the earth shook with their war cries. The din was so terrible that you could hear the battles from a thousand miles away, and the people in the southern lands would lie awake at night with their teeth chattering, listening to the unearthly noise. The winner of the Chenoo battle would leap on to one of the raging winds that blew through the land and fly off to find another monster to fight, or a trembling brave to eat.

But as he listened to the man and the woman, something very strange happened to this particular Chenoo. His icy heart was touched by their kindness. The generous welcome that they had given him had overwhelmed him completely.

10

Most of all, his heart danced for joy when the couple spoke to him gently and called him "Father." His bloodthirsty thoughts vanished. He stopped wanting to eat people. He decided then and there that, because they had been so kind to him, he wanted to stay with the man and the woman until the day he died.

And that's what he did. Much to the couple's surprise, the monster lived with them from then on. They stopped being afraid of him as they saw how friendly and helpful he had become, helping them to catch game and chop firewood. When winter came and the snow was too deep to hunt, he patiently shaped new arrows for the man, or helped the woman to decorate clothes with beads and porcupine quills. In the long winter evenings, when the couple snuggled down under thick robes by the fire, he told them magical stories, and soon they grew to love the old Chenoo as though he were a true member of their family.

When spring came again, the snow melted on the pine trees
and the river thawed, the man and the woman prepared to return to
their tribe. The Chenoo went with them, carrying the tepee on his back
and striding along with huge strides. But as they got farther and farther
southward, his steps grew shorter and he grew weaker and weaker. Because
he was a being of the north, the ice and snow had no effect on him, but as the
warm spring air wafted over him, it sapped his strength away. The woman and
the man pleaded with him to turn back, to ride the wind away to the north.
But the Chenoo had changed too much to go back to his harsh homeland;
besides, he had sworn to stay with the couple forever, and so he pressed on.
By the time they reached their tribe, the man and the woman had to carry
the old Chenoo, because he had grown so tired and weak.

When they reached the tribe, all the people gathered around the
monster in wonder. His face, which had once been terrible to look
at, had a peaceful air, and so they were not afraid of him.

In fact, everyone did their best to help the Chenoo, but he was old and tired and the warm southern air was wearing him away. At last, his frozen heart thawed out completely and the Chenoo died. But he died the happiest Chenoo in the land, because he had found something that no other Chenoo had found before — true friendship. The man and woman missed him and they never forgot their old companion. And they often laughed together when they remembered how the surprised old Chenoo had gotten himself two "children" one cold autumn day.

The Monster of the Whirlwind

Aborigine — Australian

IF YOU STAND quietly on the edge of a pond at evening time, you will often hear the croaking sound of frogs, humming their nighttime lullabies. But if a breeze should blow through the branches of the trees, or if a twig should suddenly snap, all you will hear is the "plop" of frightened frogs as they leap into the water.

Once, way back, there was a time when the frogs were bold and did not jump at every little sound. They lived in a large camp in the outback, on the edge of a slow-flowing river. There was plenty of food to eat during the daytime, and at night, the air was filled with the songs of a thousand frogs, croaking to the moon. But after a while, some of the younger frogs got tired of their mothers and their wives.

"Why should we help the women with the chores?" they grumbled to each other. "We don't want to work all day in the hot sun. We would rather lie in the cool water, eating juicy flies."

The muttering and complaining grew, until
finally, the women had had enough.

"Go, then," they said. "Set up your own camp. We can
manage very well without you!"

Joyfully, the male frogs leaped into the wide river
and swam across to the opposite bank where they
made themselves a new home. They did not
bother to do any work there at all, but dozed
or caught flies in the water all day, climbing
out to sing as the yellow moon rose in
the sky. There was no one to scold
them about the mess or
about the noise that
they made, and
they could go to
bed whenever
they liked.

But the racket that they made each evening attracted something far more frightening than the sharp words of the women frogs. Across the desert, day by day, a column of spinning dust was drawing closer and closer to the new camp. It whirled across the hard, dry land, picking up sharp stones and throwing them this way and that way. It danced around the dry bushes, plucking out their thorns and hurling them to the ground. It twirled and spun, it leaped and ran, and every day brought it a little nearer to those lazy, loud-mouthed frogs.

One evening, as the frogs gathered to sing their latest songs, a strange feeling crept over them. Each one of them felt as if he were being watched. Each one of them felt as if a pair of cold, hungry eyes was staring at him from the darkness that surrounded their camp. The frogs hopped from foot to foot and looked nervously about. A couple of them tried to sing, but their croaks sounded small in the vast night. And then a voice spoke, a voice that howled like the rushing wind. It seemed to come from everywhere and from nowhere. It whispered right into the ear of each and every frog.

"I am hungry. Bring me food."

Each frog gulped in terror. Each frog sprang to its feet and jumped into the dark river.
Each frog returned with food — some little fishes, a few water beetles, leaf mold
from the river bottom — and added it to the growing pile at the center of the camp.
No sooner had all the frogs sat down again than the food vanished, as if it had been
snatched away by invisible hands.

"What can this monster be?"
gurgled the frogs to each other
in alarm. "And where is it hiding?"

"I am in the whirlwind!" howled the voice of the unseen creature, laughing a terrible laugh.

None of the frogs dared make a sound that night, for, although it did not speak, they felt that the invisible monster was still there, watching them. Even when dawn came and the sun began its journey across the sky, they could not settle down.

As they fussed and fretted, the dreadful voice came again.

"I will depart. I will return."

The noise of howling wind echoed around the camp and Wurrawilberoo, the spirit of the whirlwind, was gone. It danced away on the shimmering air, and out onto the plains, where it played its games with the thorn bushes and the dust.

By the slow-flowing river, the frogs jumped at every sound. They hopped quickly away from flickering shadows. Their knees rattled together whenever leaves rustled or branches creaked. They listened to the noise of the running water, and their hearts beat faster whenever its notes changed. All day, they waited for the invisible monster of the whirlwind to return.

At last, the sun fell beyond the horizon. Far away on the plains, Wurrawilberoo twirled and spun, leaped and ran, and every minute brought it a little nearer to the frogs' camp. Howling with all its might, Wurrawilberoo roared up to the river again. Above the noise of the rushing wind, again the frogs heard a voice. It seemed to come from everywhere and from nowhere. It whispered right into the ear of each and every frog.

"Listen now, frogs! I am in the
whirlwind! I am in the whirlwind and
my name is . . ."

But not a single frog dared to listen to the monster's name. It was
far too powerful for a small frog to bear. To hear it would have meant
their deaths. The frogs leaped madly from their resting places. They stuffed
their toes into their ears and hurled themselves into the protecting water and
hid there for a very long time.

On the riverbank, the spirit of the whirlwind rocked from side to side with
laughter. It jumped and danced, kicking up the dust and cackling to itself.
Then it wheeled away from the water, back toward the plains.
When the frogs finally dared to poke their heads out, Wurrawilberoo
had disappeared, so they paddled silently back to their first camp.
The lady frogs were hesitant to welcome their ungrateful
husbands and sons, but hearing the horrible story of the
Wurrawilberoo, they figured that the male frogs
had learned their lesson.

Ever since that time, male and female frogs have lived together, and they have all lived in fear of the Wurrawilberoo, who they know is never far away.

That is why streams and rivers, ponds and pools, lakes and billabongs will always be the frogs' hiding places. It is why frogs are timid and will jump into the water at the slightest sound or the smallest movement.

For who can say when the spirit of the whirlwind might return?

THE ABOMINABLE SNOWMAN

Nepalese

IN A HUT high up in the snowy mountains, there once lived a poor widow woman and her son, Ramay. Although he had a kind heart and his mother loved him dearly, Ramay was an idle soul. He liked to sit outside all day, watching the birds flying and the clouds floating by. If his mother asked him to collect firewood, the hearth remained cold and cheerless. If she asked him in the morning to sweep the floor, the dust was just as thick by the time evening fell. One day, the widow finally lost her temper.

"Lazybones!" she cried in fury. "Slug-a-bed! Good-for-nothing! Out of this house you go, and don't come back until you've done an honest day's work!" And with that, she chased him from the hut, slamming the door behind him.

Ramay was very surprised by his mother's anger. He trailed off into the mountains, wondering what on earth he should do. He walked and thought and thought and walked, until he found himself far from home, with evening drawing on and his tummy rumbling like thunder.

"Perhaps there are a few crumbs to eat in my pocket," he said to himself and, as luck would have it, he found not one but three bits of stale bread. He sat down among the twisting roots of an ancient tree and got himself nice and comfy. As he was preparing to eat his meager meal, he carried on chattering to himself about the bits of bread.

"Hmm," he said. "Should I just eat one now and save the other two for later, or should I gobble up all three at once?"

Now, it just so happened that, hidden beneath the roots of the tree where Ramay sat, there was a cave where a Shokpa lived with his wife and their baby. A Shokpa is an abominable snowman, a magical creature of the mountains whose hair is as thick as a bear's to keep out the cold and as white as the snow to help him hide. The Shokpa heard Ramay talking to himself, and began to tremble with fear.

"A terrible monster is standing over our cave," he said to his wife. "I heard him trying to decide whether to munch us up one at a time or eat us all together!"

The Shokpa wife clutched her child tightly to her hairy chest and the family huddled together in fright. Their sharp teeth chattered and their bony knees clattered together like drumsticks.

"O mighty demon!" called the Shokpa. "Please, please don't eat my family, I beg you! We're very hairy and very thin and not very tasty at all! And if you promise to spare us, I'll give you my magic wand, which will grant you whatever you wish for."

Ramay leaped to his feet in amazement as the Shokpa's voice boomed up from below, but he quickly gathered his wits and replied in a growly voice, "Well, I suppose I could use your wand as a toothpick. I've just had a bite to eat, and I think that one of the goats I ate is stuck in my back molar!"

As soon as he had spoken, a wand shot up from the ground in front of him. Ramay snatched it up in delight, and set off to the house to show his mother. But before he had traveled very far, and while he was still a long way from home, the sun began to set behind the mountains. Just as he was beginning to despair of finding shelter for the night, Ramay caught sight of a little shack through the trees. An old woodcutter answered his knock and invited him in. Ramay was so excited about his adventure that he poured out the whole story to the man.

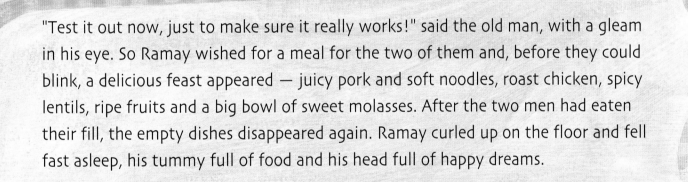

"Test it out now, just to make sure it really works!" said the old man, with a gleam in his eye. So Ramay wished for a meal for the two of them and, before they could blink, a delicious feast appeared — juicy pork and soft noodles, roast chicken, spicy lentils, ripe fruits and a big bowl of sweet molasses. After the two men had eaten their fill, the empty dishes disappeared again. Ramay curled up on the floor and fell fast asleep, his tummy full of food and his head full of happy dreams.

The next morning, he thanked the old woodcutter warmly for letting him sleep in the shack. Then he picked up the wand and made his way home, with a spring in his step and a song on his lips.

"Look, Mother!" he cried, as he strode into the widow's hut. "An abominable snowman gave me his magic wand. It grants wishes, so we will never want for anything again!"

"Abominable snowman? Magic wand?" repeated the widow in disbelief. "What nonsense! You're such a daydreamer, Ramay."

"It's true," protested her son. "Just watch this! Magic wand, grant my mother a bag of golden coins."

But nothing happened, for the crafty old woodcutter had taken the wand for himself, leaving a plain stick in its place. Ramay shook it; he tapped it on the table; he waved it wildly around his head; but still no gold appeared.

"You silly boy!" said his mother, not knowing whether to laugh or cry. "Throw away that stupid bit of wood and make yourself useful. Fetch some water from the well for me."

But Ramay was already out of the door and racing back to the Shokpa's cave, convinced that it was the monster who had tricked him. When he reached the old tree, he shouted at the roots, "Shokpa! This time, there's no escape! I'm going to eat your whole family for breakfast, you rotten trickster!"

The poor bewildered Shokpa asked Ramay to explain what on earth had happened. When he heard the sorry tale, he said, "O great demon, I didn't trick you. It must have been the old woodcutter. Take my wife's magic wand and command it to beat anyone who touches it without your permission. Then go and stay again in the old man's shack and see what happens."

29

THE GIRL WITH NO FEAR

Bantu — South African

NTOMBI, THE CHIEF'S daughter, was different from the other girls in her tribe. While they were quiet and good, the little princess ran everywhere, jumping, shouting and singing. She was cheeky to everyone and loved to argue. Ntombi was always getting into mischief, because she was a girl with no fear. The wilder the adventure, the happier she became.

Ntombi's father loved his naughty daughter, but he was afraid that one day, she would get into real trouble. Ntombi's father thought that his daughter should get married and live a quiet life, but Ntombi disagreed. When her father introduced her to handsome young princes, Ntombi just laughed.

"I don't want to get married," she would say. "I haven't seen enough of the world yet. Besides, these princes are no match for me. I only want to marry a man who has no fear."

For three years, Ntombi's father begged her to marry, and for three years, the princess refused. She wouldn't be betrothed, she said, until she had at least seen the fearsome Ilulange River with her own eyes. At first, her father wouldn't hear of it, for the river was terribly dangerous and no one ever went there. People said that the Mother of Monsters herself lived in the river and that she did not take kindly to visitors. But Ntombi pleaded so much that, in the end, the chief agreed that she could go, as long as she took the other girls with her for company.

Ntombi leaped about and whooped with joy. The other girls were not so pleased, but they loved naughty Ntombi; and so it was that, the very next morning, they all set off for the river. The girls climbed up the steep paths, singing funny songs to hide their fear. Ntombi led them on, skipping and jumping over the high rocks without a care.

At long last, they came to a deep gorge, grim and terrible. The sides were clothed with thick brush and the only sound that rose from the awful depths was the noise of a rushing river. The girls gulped, but Ntombi's eyes sparkled with delight. The princess scrambled down the steep slopes and the girls followed her down to the banks of the Ilulange River. They looked into its dark waters with a shiver. But Ntombi was disappointed.

"So this is the famous river!" she said. "I don't see what's so terrible about it. The water is a little black, perhaps, but it is probably just the high cliffs above that make it look so dark."

And with that, Ntombi took off her bracelets, and her skirt decorated with shining brass beads, and dived down, down, into the cool water.

"Come and bathe," shouted Ntombi when she popped up again. And so the girls took off their skirts and their jewelry and jumped — splosh! — into the river. Soon they were swimming and splashing and shouting, and had almost forgotten their terror. Until, that is, the littlest girl climbed out onto the bank and gave a scream.

"Someone has taken all our things!" she howled. "It must have been the Mother of Monsters. Oh, why ever did we come here?" And she began to cry.

Hastily, all the girls scrambled out of the river and clustered around the littlest girl.

"Don't cry!" said one of them. "If it was the Mother of Monsters who took our things, we should ask her nicely to return them. I am sure that she will give them back."

"Mother of Monsters!" said the littlest girl, turning to face the river. "I'm sorry! I didn't mean to disturb you — it was Ntombi's idea to come here!"

In a moment, her clothes and her bracelets came flying out of the river and landed soggily on the bank. One by one, the other girls begged for their clothes back, and each time, they flew up from the dark water and onto the bank. Finally, only Ntombi was left without her things. But a fierce frown had appeared on her proud face, and she said crossly, "Why should a princess have to plead with a river monster? You horrible old thing, I'm not afraid of you!"

36

The words were hardly out of her mouth when a
gigantic head rose out of the water and two bulging eyes glared down at the
princess. Mud poured from the monster's thick, slimy scales, and long green weeds
hung dripping from her gaping jaws. Before the princess could gather her wits and
run, the Mother of Monsters had swallowed her in one great and noisy gulp.

Screaming, Ntombi's companions scattered. They fled through the brush and didn't
stop running until they reached home, almost fainting with fright. When the chief
heard what had happened, he summoned his warriors and sent them off to rescue
the princess. But as soon as the nervous warriors reached the riverbank, the scaly
head rose from the depths again with a roar and a great gush of water, and
swallowed them all whole.

The Mother of Monsters had decided that she liked the sweet taste of humankind. She liked the taste so much, in fact, that she climbed right out of the water. Crushing bushes and trees, the monster tore up the steep sides of the gorge. She thundered her way across the countryside, looking for food. Everyone ran away as fast as they could, but it was no use. She caught the people in her terrible claws and ate them in one mouthful, with a smack of her slimy lips. The more she ate, the hungrier she felt, and soon she was gulping down everything that moved — humans, cattle, dogs and even the snarling wild cats all disappeared into her slavering jaws.

Finally, she reached the kraal of a handsome young hunter named Sobabili. Sobabili's wife had died a few years before, and his children were tending the family's cattle. Quick as a flash, the Mother of Monsters gobbled the two little children up, and all the cattle too.

When Sobabili came home from hunting, he could hardly believe his eyes. His home had been squashed flat by the monster's bulging belly, and his children and all his livestock were gone. But instead of despairing, Sobabili was furious. The monster didn't frighten him at all. He decided to find her by following the furrow that her tummy had ploughed in the ground.

After a while, a wild old elephant came charging toward him, but Sobabili wasn't afraid. Instead, he asked, "Elephant, elephant, have you seen the creature who crunched up my children and ruined my home?"

"You mean the Mother of Monsters, the Crusher of Trees?
Yes, she passed this way — keep going on!"

Sobabili thanked the elephant. He kept going until he noticed two young leopards, stalking him through the long, dry grass. But Sobabili wasn't afraid. Instead, he asked, "Leopards, leopards, have you seen the creature who crunched up my children and ruined my home?"

"You mean the Mother of Monsters, the Crusher of Trees,
Who rose from the river gnashing her jaws?
Yes, she passed this way — keep going on!"

Sobabili thanked the leopards and followed the trail until he chanced
upon a roaring lion. But Sobabili wasn't afraid. Instead, he asked,
"Lion, lion, have you seen the creature who crunched up my children
and ruined my home?"

"You mean the Mother of Monsters, the Crusher of Trees,
Who rose from the river gnashing her jaws
Because of a princess who wouldn't say 'please'?
Yes, she passed this way — keep going on!"

With a nod of thanks, Sobabili continued with his search. At last, he saw
a big, dark hill ahead of him. But then he saw that the hill had a huge head
with bulging eyes and a wide, greedy mouth. Walking toward it, he asked,
"O great one, have you seen the creature who crunched up my children
and ruined my home?"

"You mean the Mother of Monsters, the Crusher of Trees,
Who rose from the river gnashing her jaws
Because of a princess who wouldn't say 'please'?
Step close to me — I'll show you where she is."

40

And so Sobabili stepped right up to the fearsome mouth, but the monster was so full and dozy, she was too slow to snap him up. Quick as a flash, Sobabili chopped her open from end to end, and out spilled the whole countryside, alive and well. Sobabili's two children roly-polied out, followed by all the people, cattle and wild animals that the monster had eaten, including the nervous warriors. Right at the end, out plopped the willful princess.

Ntombi was very sorry indeed that all the people had been guzzled by the Mother of Monsters because of her. Her father was furious with her at first, but he couldn't stay angry for long. And when she told him that she would like to get married after all, he cheered up a great deal. For when Ntombi had plopped out of the monster's tummy and seen Sobabili standing there, she knew at once that she had found her equal. She had found a man without fear, and so she fell in love with him right away.

A great wedding feast was held and the two were married. But Ntombi went on to have a great many more adventures after that, for she was the girl with no fear, and the wilder the adventure, the happier she became.

Rona Long-Teeth

Tahitian

ON THE ISLAND of Tahiti, there once lived an evil she-monster called Rona Long-Teeth. She knew many powerful spells, and her heart was wicked through and through.

Rona Long-Teeth's home was a little hut in a clearing amongst the banana trees. She lived with her baby daughter, Hina, who was as good as her mother was bad. Every day, Rona Long-Teeth would rub the little girl's skin with sandalwood oil to make it soft and scented. Every day, she would comb Hina's long, dark hair until each strand was as smooth as water. Every day, she rolled the tips of Hina's fingers until they were more slender and delicate than any fingers you have ever seen.

Rona Long-Teeth fed Hina with the best foods so that she would grow up strong and healthy. She caught juicy crabs on the reef, and cooked their sweet meat for her daughter. As the years passed, the monster's child grew into a beautiful young woman.

But although she loved Hina, Rona Long-Teeth felt nothing for the rest of the people on the island. When the moon was full, she would creep from hut to hut, and carry off the tenderest young humans that she could find to eat. The island people lived in fear of the wicked she-monster and her pointed teeth.

One young man, whose name was Monoi, could not bear to live in fear of Rona any longer. One night, he ran away to a special place that he knew, where a high cliff stood by a shady pool. He found himself a cozy cave, which he lined with bark mats, and there he hid. He sealed up the rock with a magic song so that there was no sign of the entrance from the outside. When he wanted to leave the cave to find food or to breathe the clear morning air, he would sing the charm-song again and the rock would open.

It so happened that the shady pool was Hina's favorite place to bathe, and one day Monoi saw her swimming in the water and fell in love. He forgot his fear and left the cave to talk to her. Monoi was as handsome as Hina was beautiful, and Hina fell in love with him too. They sat by the pool all morning long, singing songs and telling each other jokes. But for all Hina's pleading, Monoi would not tell her where he lived.

"I dare not tell you, in case your mother finds me and eats me," he explained.

44

Hina was horrified. She had had no idea that Rona Long-Teeth dined on human beings. She promised never to tell her mother where Monoi lived, so he showed her the secret cave and told her that he would always come out of the rock if she stood outside and called him.

So the very next day, as soon as Rona Long-Teeth had gone to the reef, Hina gathered a basket of food, raced down to the bottom of the high cliff and sang:

"Here is your friend!
Come out and have fun.
Open the rock and we'll dance in the sun."

From inside the rock, Monoi answered jokingly:

"Where is your mother with her teeth sharp and long?
Answer me that, and I'll sing the charm-song."

"She's on the long reef, she's on the short reef,
  she's catching crabs for supper!" laughed Hina.

Then Monoi sang the charm-song, and out he sprang from the cliff. They played together all morning, and when the sun was high in the sky, they sat by the water and ate the picnic that Hina had brought.

"My heart belongs to you," said Monoi to Hina. "I'll love you forever." Then he jumped back into his hiding place and Hina hurried away. She got home just before Rona Long-Teeth returned with a basketful of crabs. But Rona was as sharp as her pointed teeth, and she noticed how much food was missing from the hut.

"Hina has eaten like a little pig today!" she muttered. "She has gobbled enough food for two. Something is strange here, and I mean to find out what."

So the very next morning, the crafty monster lay down on her sleeping mat. "I don't feel well," she groaned. "I think that I will stay here and sleep until I feel better. My poor old legs are too weak to walk to the reef today."

Hina was so eager to see Monoi again that she waited until her mother began to snore, and then she gathered up a picnic and ran to the cliff. But Rona Long-Teeth was only pretending to be asleep. Quickly, she jumped up and followed Hina to the shady pool, where she watched her daughter sing and Monoi leap from the rock. Rona Long-Teeth was furious. Her blood boiled and she ground her teeth in rage.

"Young he looks, and tasty too," she snarled to herself. "I shall eat him, by and by."

And she took herself off home. But that night, she said to her daughter, "Hina dear, I think that I will go fishing by torchlight. When I get back, we shall have an early breakfast of breadfruit and yams and delicious fresh fish."

"I'm glad that you feel better, Mother," replied Hina with a smile. "And fresh fish for breakfast sounds delightful."

Off went Rona Long-Teeth, tiptoeing through the darkness, until she came to Monoi's cliff. There, she sang as sweetly as she could:

"Here is your friend!
Come out and have fun.
Open the rock and we'll dance all night long."

But Monoi wasn't fooled. "You aren't Hina!" he shouted. "You're Rona Long-Teeth, and I'm not coming out!"

But Rona didn't care, for she was a powerful enchantress and she knew a magic word that would open the cave.

48

"Vahia!" she screamed, and the rock split open with a sound like thunder. In rushed the she-monster. The teeth in her mouth grew longer and longer, and fangs appeared all over her — on her chin and on her elbows and on her knees and on her belly, until she was covered from head to toe in big, sharp teeth. Before Monoi could so much as squeak, she had devoured him, every last bit. Every last bit, that is, except for his heart, for his heart belonged to Hina and it hid itself behind a rock. Then Rona Long-Teeth went off to the reef, to fish by torchlight.

Meanwhile, in the hut, Hina's heart gave a great lurch. She knew that something terrible had happened to her friend. She ran to the cliff and into the cave, and heard Monoi's heart call out to her. Straight away, she picked it up and placed it next to her own heart. Then she ran home.

"Find a stem of a banana tree that is as tall as you are and cut it down," whispered the heart to Hina. "Lay it on your sleeping mat, with a coconut in the place where your head would rest, and cover the plants with a soft white cloth."

Hina did as the heart told her. It looked as though she was fast asleep in bed.

"Now fly like a bird to Chief Noa's house. Tell him everything that has happened, and ask him to get his spear ready."

Hina ran across the dark island as fast as her legs could carry her.

Now, long after midnight, when all of her fishing torches had burned down, Rona Long-Teeth came home. She threw down her catch and called to Hina, "Here's some fish for you!" But the shape in the bed did not stir.

"Ah, poor child, she is tired out," said Rona Long-Teeth, and she lit a little fire. After a while, she called, "Hina, come and sing to me while I cook." But the shape in the bed did not stir.

"Ah, poor child, I will let her sleep a while longer," muttered the wicked monster. When the fish were cooked to a crisp, Rona Long-Teeth called, "Hina, get up, the meal is ready!" But the shape in the bed did not stir.

Rona Long-Teeth went over to the bed and pulled off the soft tapa cloth. When she saw the coconut and the banana tree lying on Hina's sleeping mat, she was filled with rage. She knew that she had been tricked, and that her daughter had fled long ago.

As the dawn rose, Rona Long-Teeth raced across the island. Everywhere, she screamed, "Where is Hina? Where is my daughter?" The people were very afraid. They pointed toward the chief's house, and Rona Long-Teeth ran in through the door. When she saw her daughter there, the teeth in her mouth grew longer and longer, and fangs appeared all over her — on her chin and on her elbows and on her knees and on her belly, until she was covered from head to toe in big, sharp teeth. But Chief Noa was ready with his spear, as the heart had told him to be, and before she could chomp Hina in two, Rona Long-Teeth met her end.

Then Chief Noa took Monoi's heart from Hina and gave it to his best enchanter. The enchanter made a new body for Monoi and set the heart inside it. Monoi and Hina fell into each other's arms, and the chief married them on the spot. And, freed from their fear of the monstrous Rona Long-Teeth, everyone on the island lived in peace and plenty for the rest of their days.

THe FeatHered Ogre

Italian

LONG AGO IN a country far away, the king fell sick. The royal doctor was summoned to his bedside. He made the king say "Ah" and he counted the beats of the king's heart, and finally he shook his head.

"Only a magic feather from the ogre's back can cure you, Sire!"

All of the noble knights and ladies gasped in horror. The feathered ogre, who lived on an island far to the north, was feared throughout the kingdom. Every year, he would jump into a boat and come to the mainland. There, he would capture one hundred of the most tasty and tender young men and women and take them back to the island to put in his pantry. Last year, he had even snatched the king's eldest daughter, who had been visiting her aunt in the north. Many brave men had set out to the ogre's lair to put an end to his gruesome habit, but none had ever returned.

The noble ruler gave a huge sigh.

"Let it be known that whoever brings a feather from the ogre's back will have the hand of my beautiful younger daughter in marriage and half of my kingdom to call his own," the king commanded.

But in his heart, he despaired, because the journey was so frightening. And whether they were old or young, brave or cowardly, all of the people agreed with their king. Plucking a feather right from the evil ogre's back was utterly impossible. No one would risk being the next tasty morsel to be put in the ogre's pantry.

No one? Well, perhaps there was one person who was brave enough to go. Pírolo, the youngest of the king's gardeners, had had enough of weeding the royal potato patch and picking fat caterpillars off the kingly cabbages. When he heard about the reward, a dreamy look came into his eyes. A wild adventure, half a kingdom . . . the only bad part was having to marry the younger princess, who always made faces at him from the palace windows. Still, Pírolo threw down his spade, found himself a stout staff, and walked off to the north.

Pírolo traveled for many days over hill and dale. He walked through lush valleys where the grass was as soft as silk and as green as a frog. He walked over rocky cliffs where the rough stones were as lumpy and twisted as a witch's nose.

Finally, he reached the shore at the end of the kingdom. There before
him lay the sea and over the sea lay the feathered ogre's island.

As he stood there, wondering to himself how he might get across, Pírolo
heard the splash of oars and a person sighing long, sad sighs. An ancient
wooden boat was drifting toward him over the waves. In the boat sat
the oldest man that Pírolo had ever seen. His face was as wrinkled as
a raisin and the tip of his long, white beard trailed over the side of
the boat into the salty water.

"Good day, Ferryman!" called Pírolo cheerily as the boat reached the
shore. "Will you row me over to the feathered ogre's island?"

The ferryman looked at Pírolo with his tired eyes. When he spoke, his voice was the weariest sound in the world.

"Traveler, I have rowed from shore to shore for a thousand years. I am worn to the bone, but the feathered ogre has placed an enchantment on me and I cannot get out of this boat. It doesn't matter to me, sir, whether there is a passenger in it or not."

Pírolo jumped into the little boat, shaking his head at the ferryman's gloomy tale.

When they reached the island, the ferryman pointed to a huge wooden door set into the cliff nearby. Not knowing what else to do, Pírolo took a deep breath, and striding across the sand, he banged on the door with his staff.

After a while, the door creaked slowly open. Pírolo raised the stout staff again, ready to give the ogre a bop on the nose. But instead of an ugly monster, a beautiful girl with bright blue eyes stood behind the door. She looked at Pírolo with a puzzled frown.

"You're not the feathered ogre!" she said. "Who are you, and why are you here?"

When Pírolo had explained everything to the girl, she said in surprise, "Why, the king is my father! That wicked old ogre captured me last year when I was visiting my auntie. He didn't eat me, because I offered to keep his house spick and span for him. I helped the other people to escape from his pantry and fed the ogre mutton instead. Now I want to go home too. If you help me to find the way, I'll get a feather for you."

Of course, Pírolo agreed.

"Come into the kitchen and hide under the table," said the princess. "The ogre will be back soon!"

57

No sooner had Pírolo dived under the table than the door burst open and in strode the feathered ogre. His horrible scowling face was as scrunched as a rotten cabbage.

"Where's my tea?" he shouted.

"Here it is, ogre dear," said the princess. "You munched the last man yesterday, so it's just delicious dumplings tonight."

"Bah!" roared the ogre, stuffing all of the dumplings into his mouth at once. "Tomorrow, I will catch more tasty human beans for my supper."

And then the feathered ogre wiped his chin on one feathery arm and started to snigger. "Harg harg harg! Every time I sit in the boat with that old ferryman, I split my sides. If only he knew!" And he wiped a tear of laughter from his eye.

"If only he knew what, ogre dear?" asked the princess.

"If only he knew how easy it is for him to escape from my magic! If he gave his passenger the oars to hold, then jumped out quicksticks from the boat, he would be as free as the air. The passenger would be stuck in his place instead, rowing from shore to shore until doomsday. Harg harg harg!"

Under the table, Pírolo was listening carefully.

"Ogre dear, you look tired," murmured the princess thoughtfully. "Why don't you have a little nap?"

"Mm," said the feathered ogre with a great yawn, putting his head down on the table. "Good idea. I'm tired out from ogreing all day."

The girl stroked the ogre's feathers and sang to him until he fell into a deep sleep. As soon as he began to snore, she quickly pulled a magic feather from his back and threw it under the table to Pírolo.

"Ow!" howled the ogre, waking up. "I've been stung!"

"There, there, ogre dear," the princess soothed. "It was just a little spark from the fire that singed one of your pretty feathers. Go back to sleep."

"Hmm," said the ogre sleepily, putting his head back on the table. Soon he was snoring again.

"Quick!" whispered the princess to Pírolo. "Now's our chance — run!"

Hand in hand, the pair ran across the cave. They opened the huge door and rushed outside into the daylight. But the door slammed shut with a loud bang and, as they ran toward the ferryman's boat, they heard the ogre wake up with a roar of rage.

"Row, Ferryman, row!" cried Pírolo as they hurled themselves into the boat. Behind them, the door of the cave burst open and out charged the ogre.

"Come back!" he bellowed, hopping up and down in the sand.

But the ferryman rowed as if the sea was on fire, and Pírolo and the princess jumped out, safe at the other side. They told the ferryman how to escape from his curse and the first smile in a thousand years spread slowly across his face.

Then Pírolo and the princess ran homeward, clutching the precious feather. Over hill and dale they dashed until finally they reached the palace. The magic feather cured the king's illness in a second, and he was so happy to see his elder daughter again that he danced a jig around the throne room. He granted Pírolo half of his kingdom, and let him marry the elder daughter instead of the younger one, so everyone was happy.

Everyone? Well, everyone except for the wicked feathered ogre. For as Pírolo and the princess ran home, the ferryman rowed back to the island where the monster leaped into the boat with a curse and a roar.

"I'll catch that nasty pair, see if I don't," he shouted. "Row faster!"

The ogre was so angry that he didn't notice that the ferryman was smiling as he said, "Why don't you take the oars? A mighty ogre like you could row much faster than an old man like me."

Not realizing for a moment that the ferryman knew the secret, the ogre grabbed the oars and sent the boat skimming over the waves like a bird. But before he could get out at the other side, the ferryman jumped out of the boat into the shallow water.

"Ha ha!" he laughed, clicking his heels in the air with delight. "I'm free! As free as the air!"

And he ran away over the pebbly beach.

The feathered ogre gave such a howl of horror that Pírolo and the princess heard it, far away in the palace. For now the ogre was cursed to row the boat from shore to shore until doomsday. And as far as I know, he's rowing still.